Ontario

Ontario

Michael Barnes

Lerner Publications Company

LIBRARY OF CONGRESS
CATALOGING-IN-PUBLICATION DATA

Barnes, Michael.
    Ontario/by Michael Barnes
        p. cm. —(Hello Canada)
    Includes index.
    ISBN 0–8225–2754–5 (lib. bdg.)
    1. Ontario—Juvenile literature. I. Title. II. Series.
F1057.4.B37 1995
971.3—dc20   94–20253
                                                  CIP
                                                   AC

Manufactured in the United States of America

1 2 3 4 5 6 – I/JR – 00 99 98 97 96 95

Cover photograph courtesy of Industry, Science, and Technology Canada. Background photo by R. Chen/ SuperStock.

The glossary that begins on page 72 gives definitions of words shown in **bold type** in the text.

Senior Editor
Gretchen Bratvold
Editor
Elizabeth Weiss
Photo Researcher
Cindy Hartmon
Designer
Steve Foley

Our thanks to the following people for their help in preparing this book: Paul McIlroy, Reference Archivist from Archives of Ontario, and Judy Murdoch, consultant.

 This book is printed on acid-free, recyclable paper.

Contents

Fun Facts

CN Tower

🍁 At Niagara Falls, on the border between Ontario and New York State, more than six million cubic feet (169,000 cubic meters) of water spill over the falls each minute. That's enough water to fill 62 Olympic-size swimming pools every minute!

🍁 Scientists believe that a huge explosion helped form northern Ontario's mineral-rich Sudbury Basin. The blast may have happened when a giant meteor from outer space crashed there almost two billion years ago. Or it may have been the fiery work of ancient volcanoes.

🍁 The CN (Canadian National) Tower in Toronto, Ontario, is the tallest building in the world. It reaches 1,814 feet (553 meters) into the sky.

Petroglyphs

🍁 All aboard! From 1926 to 1967, trains were used as classrooms for students in remote areas of northern Ontario. Teachers in these schools-on-wheels helped children at each stop learn math and reading skills.

🍁 Hundreds of images of people, animals, and birds are etched on limestone rocks near Peterborough, Ontario. These ancient pictures, called petroglyphs, were carved by Native peoples almost one thousand years ago.

🍁 Ontario's Manitoulin Island, in Lake Huron, is the world's largest island in a lake. The island covers 1,068 square miles (2,766 square kilometers).

Hi! My name is Barkley. As you read *Ontario,* I will be helping you make sense of some of the maps and charts that appear in the book.

A Place of Shining Water

Wind rustling through the leaves of a maple tree. The haunting call of a loon. A splash as a lake trout jumps. These are some of the sounds you might hear while sitting on the shore of one of Ontario's 250,000 lakes. The name *Ontario,* which comes from an Iroquois Indian language, means "beautiful lake" or "shining water."

Many of Ontario's sparkling lakes were formed about 10,000 years ago, when much of North America was covered by **glaciers.** These massive sheets of thick ice slid across the land, and like giant bulldozers, scooped out chunks of earth. Over time, melting ice and snow filled the large holes with water, creating lakes.

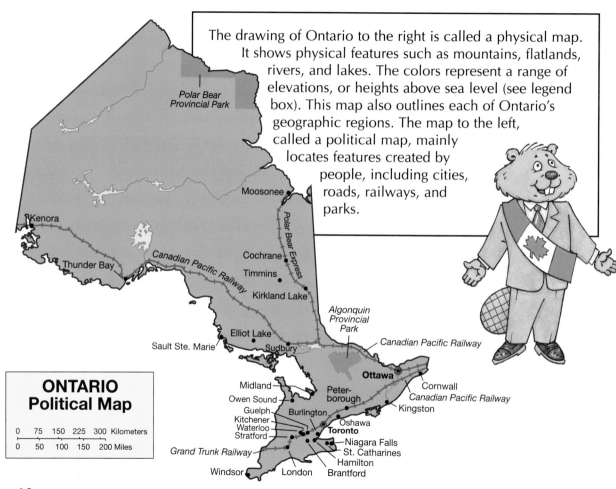

The drawing of Ontario to the right is called a physical map. It shows physical features such as mountains, flatlands, rivers, and lakes. The colors represent a range of elevations, or heights above sea level (see legend box). This map also outlines each of Ontario's geographic regions. The map to the left, called a political map, mainly locates features created by people, including cities, roads, railways, and parks.

Polar Bear Provincial Park

Moosonee

Kenora

Polar Bear Express

Thunder Bay

Canadian Pacific Railway

Cochrane

Timmins

Kirkland Lake

Algonquin Provincial Park

Elliot Lake

Sault Ste. Marie

Sudbury

Canadian Pacific Railway

Ottawa

ONTARIO
Political Map

0	75	150	225	300	Kilometers
0	50	100	150	200	Miles

Midland

Owen Sound

Guelph

Kitchener

Waterloo

Stratford

Burlington

Peter-borough

Cornwall

Canadian Pacific Railway

Kingston

Oshawa

Toronto

Niagara Falls

St. Catharines

Hamilton

Brantford

Grand Trunk Railway

Windsor

London

10

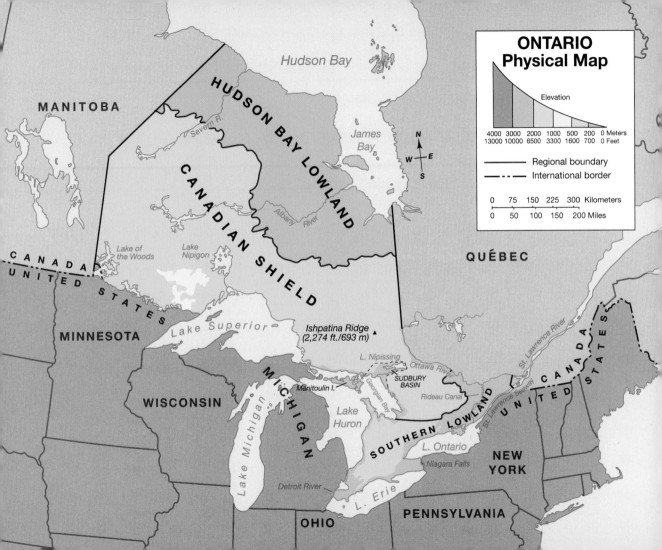

ONTARIO
Physical Map

Elevation

| 4000 | 3000 | 2000 | 1000 | 500 | 200 | 0 Meters |
| 13000 | 10000 | 6500 | 3300 | 1600 | 700 | 0 Feet |

Regional boundary
International border

| 0 | 75 | 150 | 225 | 300 | Kilometers |
| 0 | 50 | 100 | 150 | 200 | Miles |

MANITOBA

Hudson Bay

HUDSON BAY LOWLAND

James
Bay

Severn R.

CANADIAN SHIELD

Albany River

QUÉBEC

CANADA
UNITED STATES

Lake of
the Woods

Lake
Nipigon

MINNESOTA

Lake Superior

Ishpatina Ridge
(2,274 ft./693 m)

L. Nipissing

Ottawa River

St. Lawrence River

SUDBURY
BASIN

Rideau Canal

St. Lawrence River

C A N A D A
U N I T E D   S T A T E S

WISCONSIN

MICHIGAN

Manitoulin I.

Georgian Bay

Lake
Huron

SOUTHERN LOWLAND

St. Lawrence Seaway

Lake Michigan

L. Ontario

NEW
YORK

Niagara Falls

Detroit River

L. Erie

OHIO

PENNSYLVANIA

N
W   E
S

Moraines, or deposits of earth and stones left by glaciers, wrinkle parts of southern Ontario's land.

The glaciers also helped form the **Great Lakes.** Four of these five bodies of water lap against Ontario's shores. Lakes Huron, Erie, and Ontario surround southwestern Ontario. To the northwest lies Lake Superior.

Across the Great Lakes are some of Ontario's neighbors—the U.S. states of Wisconsin, Michigan, Ohio, Pennsylvania, and New York. The state of Minnesota and the province of Manitoba hug Ontario's northwestern edge.

To Ontario's far north is Hudson Bay. Whales, walrus, and seals swim in this icy saltwater sea. Polar bears lumber along the shores. At the southern end, James Bay dips between Ontario and its eastern neighbor, Québec.

As the second largest province in Canada, Ontario is almost twice the size of the state of Texas. The European countries of France and Germany could almost fit inside Ontario's borders.

At Polar Bear Park, wildlife lovers may catch a glimpse of the huge white animals. The wilderness area hugs the rugged shores of the Hudson and James Bays.

Many of the ancient boulders on the surface of the rocky Canadian Shield are millions of years old.

Most of the province's land is a vast wilderness that Ontarians think of as northern Ontario. This region extends north and west from Lake Nipissing all the way to the Manitoba border. The area contains most of the province's two biggest geographic regions— the Canadian Shield and the Hudson Bay Lowland. Although northern Ontario is huge, only 10 percent of Ontarians call it home.

The Canadian Shield is Ontario's largest geographic region, covering more than half of the province. The Shield extends from parts of southern Ontario all the way to the province's far northwestern edges. In this rocky, mineral-rich region, miners dig for nickel and copper around Sudbury, a northern city that sits in the Sudbury Basin. Timmins and Kirkland Lake are other major mining towns.

With many thick forests, the Canadian Shield provides timber for Ontario's logging industry. Mills in cities such as Kenora and Thunder Bay process logs into pulp and paper. The region's wildlife, scenic lakes, and winding rivers attract hunters and tourists.

The Hudson Bay Lowland, Ontario's northernmost region, curves around the Hudson and James Bays. Here mossy bogs, or **muskegs,** cover much of the land. In this cold, swampy stretch of wilderness, trees have trouble growing to their full size. **Permafrost,** or soil that is always frozen, lies beneath some areas. Very few people inhabit this flat, rugged region.

Southern Ontario, on the other hand, is full of people and big cities. The capital of the province—Toronto—lies in the south on the shore of Lake Ontario. Ottawa, the national capital, is located in the south, too. Many southern residents work in offices, in the government, or in bustling automobile factories.

Within southern Ontario lies the province's third geographic region—the Southern Lowland. It extends from the Ottawa River in the southeast to the southwestern tip of the province. This region, with its valleys and gently rolling hills, contains Ontario's most fertile soil. Farmers there grow fruits, grains, vegetables, and tobacco. Dairy cows and beef cattle graze on the region's pastures.

The deep, rich soil of southern Ontario helps corn and other crops thrive.

Ships carrying products such as iron ore and grain from Ontario's ports pass through the Saint Lawrence Seaway (left), **one of the world's busiest shipping routes. Nearby, on the Niagara River, Niagara Falls** (facing page) **is Ontario's most popular tourist spot.**

Several large waterways, including the Ottawa and Saint Lawrence Rivers, flow through southeastern Ontario. In the north, the Severn and Albany Rivers cross the Hudson Bay Lowland and empty into the Hudson and James Bays. Used for travel and for trade, all of these waterways have played important roles in Ontario's history.

An international trade route called the Saint Lawrence Seaway runs along the Saint Lawrence River and through some of the Great Lakes. On the seaway, canals allow ships to bypass dangerous river rapids. **Locks** raise or lower water levels to help boats travel through steep parts of the waterway. Huge freighters using the seaway haul grain, minerals, and other cargoes from Ontario's ports to the Atlantic Ocean and beyond.

Another important river, the Niagara, forms part of the border between Canada and the United States. Along the river, the famous Niagara Falls plunge over the rim of a high limestone cliff. Water from the Niagara and from many of Ontario's other rivers is harnessed for **hydropower.** Ontario's hydroelectric plants produce about one-fourth of the province's electricity.

The bodies of water bordering Ontario affect the province's climate. Winter is longer and colder in areas near Hudson Bay. Strong winds whip across the frozen bay, keeping winter temperatures at −8° F (−22° C). In summer, the average temperature along Hudson Bay is only 54° F (12° C).

Winds blowing off the Great Lakes warm cities along Ontario's southern shores. Winter temperatures are milder in the south than in the far north, but the season is harsh and stormy throughout Ontario. Yearly snowfall can reach as high as 98 inches (250 centimeters) in the Snow Belt—areas east of Georgian Bay off Lake Huron. Summer temperatures usually stay above 68° F (20° C) in Toronto and in Ottawa. Windsor, in southwestern Ontario, has the warmest weather.

Each fall and spring, flocks of loudly honking Canada geese soar over Ontario. Springtime also brings newly hatched birds, such as finches and ruffed grouse. During summer, red foxes, black bears, and white-tailed deer take shelter in the province's shady woodlands.

During winter, ice-skaters (facing page) *glide across the frozen Rideau Canal in Ottawa. The white trillium* (above), *the province's official flower, blooms during springtime.*

Iroquoian Indians (inset) *lived in rectangular homes called longhouses* (above) *that were made from tree saplings and cedar bark.*

20

Native Peoples and Newcomers

As the last glaciers melted, the climate warmed and moss plants sprang up in what is now Ontario. Hungry elk and caribou moved there, followed by early hunters who stalked the herds for meat. Nearly 4,000 years later, shady pine forests and sparkling rivers covered the land. Native peoples, or Indians, settled the area to hunt, fish, and gather food. Over time, more and more Indians arrived.

By A.D. 900, Indians in what is now Ontario belonged to two main groups that each spoke their own language. Iroquoian speakers, such as the Huron, Neutral, and Erie nations, lived in large villages in what is now southern Ontario. They planted corn and hunted. Storing the extra crops and dried meat, the Indians had enough food to last through the long winters and to trade with their neighbors.

Many Algonquian groups built cone-shaped homes using saplings and animal hides.

To the north, Algonquian speakers included the Ojibwa, Algonquin, and Cree nations. They lived on land that was too harsh and rocky for farming. In the thick forests, hunters killed large game animals, trapped beavers, and speared fish in streams and rivers. The Indians also gathered roots, berries, and wild rice for food. The Algonquian speakers traded meat and animal hides with their Iroquoian neighbors in exchange for corn.

One of the Iroquoian-speaking groups, the Hurons, soon became the largest Indian nation near the Great Lakes. The vast territory of the Hurons spread along the southeastern shore of Georgian Bay. Fields of corn, squash, beans, and sunflowers provided food for thousands of Huron people.

In 1610 a young Frenchman named Étienne Brûlé journeyed toward Georgian Bay. He had been sent by Samuel de Champlain, the leader of the French **colony,** or settlement, of New France (present-day Québec). While claiming new lands for the French king, Brûlé made friends with the Hurons. The Indians helped New France start a fur trade in the Great Lakes region.

Étienne Brûlé was only 17 years old when he set foot on Huron land. He most likely was the first European to see Lakes Huron, Ontario, and Superior.

23

Lost at Sea

In 1610 Henry Hudson set out in search of a northern water route from Europe to Asia. After a few months, the British captain guided his ship into a foggy, salt-water sea. Hudson thought he had reached the Pacific Ocean. Despite the cold weather and the ice forming on the water, Hudson ordered his crew to press on. The crew was unaware that they were charting the shorelines of what is now northern Ontario.

By the time the crew had reached the bay's southern end, frozen seas prevented the craft from sailing back out. Forced to spend winter aboard the ship, the men were starving and chilled to the bone. In the spring, the ice started to melt and the captain once again set a course for Asia.

The men were so angry with Hudson for getting the ship stuck and for making them continue the long, dangerous journey that they rebelled. The rebels put Hudson and a few loyal crew members in a small rowboat, then sailed away from what is now known as Hudson Bay. No one knows for sure what happened to the rowboat and its men.

The Hurons acted as go-betweens—they traded with Algonquian hunters to get beaver furs, which they then traded with the French. The French fur traders were called *coureurs de bois,* or "runners of the woods." They gave the Hurons blankets and other European goods in exchange for furs. The French traders sold the pelts to France to be made into fashionable hats.

Soon more French people headed to the Hurons' land. Some of these newcomers were Catholic **missionaries,** who were eager to spread their religion. In 1639 they built a mission named Sainte Marie near Georgian Bay, where they taught their faith to the Hurons.

The missionaries and fur traders unknowingly brought new diseases to the Hurons and to other Indian nations in

Catholic priests arrived to teach their religion to the Hurons. But many of the Indians did not want to learn a new religion.

what is now Ontario. Because Native peoples had never before been exposed to illnesses such as smallpox, thousands died.

Many other Hurons were killed in warfare with the Iroquois. This group of five nations in what is now New York competed for the fur trade. The Iroquois tried to disrupt the French fur business by attacking French traders who were traveling on the Saint Lawrence River. In 1648 and 1649, the Iroquois raided Huron settlements and killed many villagers.

But the attacks did not stop New France's fur trade. Instead French traders built trading posts near the Ottawa River and along Lakes Huron and Superior. Two adventurous French fur traders, Médard Chouart des Groseilliers and Pierre-Esprit Radisson, wanted to trade as far north as Hudson Bay. Without getting permission from French officials, the two traders led an expedition to collect furs in the far north. The men were forced to pay a heavy fine when they returned.

Angry at this punishment, the traders went to the British king. He and a group of rich British men agreed to help start trading posts near Hudson Bay. They founded the Hudson's Bay Company in 1670. Britain claimed all of the land that held rivers draining into the bay, naming this vast area Rupert's Land.

The British made friends with Cree Indians in the region. Expert trappers, the Cree supplied the British traders with beaver pelts. The furs were sent directly to Britain by way of Hudson Bay. Soon the British fur trade was doing so well that French traders feared they would lose business.

With a water route from Hudson Bay to Britain, British fur traders in what is now northern Ontario built up a thriving business.

For many years, the French and the British fought over the fur trade. Battles between the French and the British erupted on land and in the bay. In 1713 the French signed a **treaty,** agreeing to give the British control of Rupert's Land.

But disputes between France and Britain continued. The two countries fought in Europe as well as in North America. In 1763 France lost the Seven Years' War (also called the French and Indian War). The French were forced to accept British rule in most of their North American settlements, including what is now Ontario.

Soon trouble was brewing for Britain farther south. Several British colonies along the Atlantic coast were demanding the freedom to make their own laws. With help from the Iroquois, Britain went to war against these colonists in 1775. When the colonists won the Revolutionary War, they formed their own country—the United States of America—in 1783.

Joseph Brant was an Iroquois leader who fought alongside British soldiers during the Revolutionary War. In return for the Iroquois' loyalty, Britain gave Brant's people land near the Grand River in what is now southwestern Ontario. By 1785 about 1,800 Native peoples lived on this reserve.

After the war, many settlers in the United States still felt loyal to Britain and wanted to live in a British colony. Called **Loyalists,** these people moved to British North America (present-day Canada). Most settled on land near the shores of Lakes Ontario and Erie.

At the same time, thousands of Iroquois came to British North America. These Indians had been driven from their homelands in the United States for siding with Britain. The British government offered the Iroquois Loyalists some territory north of Lake Erie. This land became an Iroquois **reserve.**

Meanwhile, many white Loyalists were unhappy. Even though they lived under British rule, the people had to follow French laws. Britain feared that changing the laws would anger the thousands of French-speaking settlers who lived east of the Ottawa River in what is now Québec.

To please both the British and the French settlers, Britain passed the Constitutional Act of 1791. This law split the British colony into Upper Canada (now southern Ontario) and Lower Canada (present-day southern

Québec). Officials in Upper Canada replaced French laws with British ones.

More people came to Upper Canada when the governor offered territory around the Great Lakes. In exchange for plots of land, settlers built farms, fences, and roads. Many of the newcomers were **immigrants** from the United States. To open more land for settlement, the British government began moving most of the region's Native peoples to northern reserves. In exchange for leaving their land, the Indians received money and goods.

By the early 1800s, nearly 70,000 settlers lived in Upper Canada. New cabins and farms dotted the land. Soon thousands of British, Scottish, and Irish immigrants began to arrive, setting up their own small communities or moving to Upper Canada's growing towns.

The War of 1812 was fought by the United States and Britain. After war was declared, U.S. officials planned an invasion of British-controlled Upper Canada. Convinced that the colony was an easy target, American soldiers marched toward Upper Canada prepared for a quick victory. But for two years, fierce battles raged on land and at sea. By 1814 both sides were tired of fighting and agreed to make peace. As a result, Upper Canada remained firmly British and its settlers were more determined than ever to defend their land.

Immigrants and Industry

Irish immigrants

Many of the European immigrants in Upper Canada had left the crowded cities of their homelands to begin new lives. Some of the newcomers got jobs building roads. Others started farms to grow wheat, apples, or peaches or to raise dairy cows.

When British immigrants also went to neighboring Lower Canada, many of the French people there began to worry. They did not want to lose their laws and customs to the British.

Following the North Star

In 1833 Britain outlawed slavery in all of its colonies, including British North America. As a result, Upper Canada was seen as a place of freedom for many slaves who escaped from the United States.

These African Americans headed north on the Underground Railroad, a secret network of people who risked their lives to help fleeing slaves. Traveling mostly at night with only the moon and stars to light their way, the slaves sneaked through swamps and hid in homes or barns. All the while, they listened for barking dogs, which signaled that officials were on their trail.

Many routes carried the slaves to freedom. Over the years, thousands of African Americans crossed the Detroit River, landing on the southwestern shores of Upper Canada. Some slaves were smuggled onto boats and carried across Lake Ontario. No matter what path they took, the slaves followed the bright light of the North Star, which guided them north to freedom.

People in Upper Canada had worries, too. They felt that the British governor and his council ignored the peoples' needs. Rebellions against the government took place in both Upper and Lower Canada in the 1830s. British soldiers quickly defeated the rebels.

Then Britain decided to unite the two colonies in 1841. Upper Canada was called Canada West, and Lower Canada was renamed Canada East. Together they became the Province of Canada, ruled by one British governor. But some people continued to push for political change. In 1848 the Province of Canada achieved **responsible government** (self-government) in local affairs.

By this time, immigrants in Canada West had built canals to improve trade routes. The canals allowed ships to

Loggers in the north relied on horses to pull loads of newly cut timber.

bypass river rapids and to travel from one Great Lake to the next. Steamships carrying wheat and cattle could now reach ports by more direct routes.

Many of the ships also hauled timber, since logging had become a big business. In fact, lumber and wheat now earned more money for the colony than the fur trade did. Fewer people made a living by selling pelts, though the fur trade continued in the far north.

THE GOVERNOR'S INSPECTION

The morning started out just like any other workday at the Moose Factory, a trading post near James Bay. Located on an island in Moose River, the post was owned and controlled by the Hudson's Bay Company. The year was 1849.

Traders were busy repairing their birchbark canoes and cleaning fish. Inside the post, a Cree trapper looked over some kettles and knives. On the counter lay glossy beaver furs that had been stretched flat and dried in the sun. The manager, or factor, was counting the pelts and recording the number of goods traded with Native trappers.

Suddenly the sound of bagpipes in the distance sent shivers through the traders. The music signaled the arrival of Governor George Simpson, who had come to inspect the post. Swift paddlers steadied Sir George's boat as he stepped ashore. A cold draft blew through the trading post when the powerful governor opened the door.

The factor grew tense as Sir George began to make notes in a leather-bound journal. Was the governor angry? People said that he used the journal for recording things that did not please him. The factor hoped that the traders had gathered enough furs and that the post appeared tidy and well run.

He waited anxiously as the governor checked the post's accounts. "Everything appears in order," said Sir George as he headed out the door. "The company will be pleased."

The traders watched Sir George's canoe as it sped away and wondered if the next post was ready for inspection.

A train chugs along southern Ontario's countryside past the scenic Niagara Falls.

In the 1840s, Britain limited the amount of lumber and wheat it bought from the Province of Canada. So Canada West began shipping large amounts of wheat and timber to the United States. With the money earned from trading with the United States, Canada West decided to build better trade routes.

Since canals froze during the winter, Canada West needed transportation routes that could be used in all kinds of weather. Railroads were the answer. In the 1850s, immigrant workers helped build tracks from Niagara Falls to Windsor. By 1860 the Grand Trunk Railway linked Canada West to the city of Montréal in Canada East. New towns sprang up along the tracks.

Soon Canada West had thousands more residents than neighboring Canada East. With more people, Canada West demanded more control in running the colony. But French people in Canada East did not want to lose the power to make decisions about their land, schools, and culture.

To settle the dispute, politicians from both colonies worked out a plan called the British North America Act of 1867. The act made Canada West and Canada East into separate provinces, with their own local governments. Canada West was renamed Ontario, and Canada East became known as Québec.

Two colonies farther east—New Brunswick and Nova Scotia—also signed the British North America Act. Under **Confederation,** the four colonies united to form a single nation—the Dominion of Canada. Ottawa became the capital of the new nation. In this city, the national government made laws that still had to be approved by the king or queen of Britain.

In 1867 John Sandfield Macdonald became the first premier of the newly established province.

To build tracks across the north, railroad workers had to blast through the region's thick rock (right). *Little did they know that beneath the ground lay rich stores of minerals. Soon miners* (facing page, top and bottom) *began drilling for gold, silver, and iron ore in the region.*

The Dominion wanted to gain new territory and bought Rupert's Land from the Hudson's Bay Company. The vast northern lands around Hudson Bay became part of Ontario. Gradually, Ontario's western boundary was pushed to what is now the Manitoba border.

The Canadian Pacific and other railroads connected northern Ontario with the rest of the province. As workers laid tracks, they discovered rich deposits of minerals in the region. Soon many northerners got jobs mining copper in

towns such as Sudbury. Factory workers manufactured the iron and steel that was used for building and repairing Ontario's trains.

By the early 1900s, other industries in northern Ontario were booming. Loggers cut down trees and sent the timber to huge pulp and paper mills for grinding. Built near rivers, many of these mills used waterpower to run equipment and to provide electricity. Hydropower was soon used to produce electricity for southern Ontario's big cities.

In the early 1900s, Slavic immigrants (left) *took jobs building railways, while many Jewish newcomers* (right) *found jobs in factories around Toronto.*

By this time, the southern cities were very crowded. Thousands of immigrants had arrived by steamship to take jobs in growing factories. At the same time, many Ontarians gave up farming and moved to Toronto, Hamilton, and other cities. These people hoped that factory jobs would earn them more money than farming had.

During World War I (1914–1918), even more cropland was abandoned when farmers were sent to fight overseas. With fewer people working the land, many farm communities grew poor. Some farmers formed a group called the United Farmers of Ontario, which worked to improve schools and roads in rural areas.

By the 1930s, Ontario and the rest of the world had fallen into a deep economic slump called the Great Depression. All over the province, people lost their jobs when factories, mills, and mining and lumber camps closed. With the outbreak of World War II in 1939, many of the plants reopened. Ontarians headed back to work to produce tanks and weapons.

Workers in Ontario assembled fighter planes during World War II.

In 1991 native leaders and the premier of Ontario signed an agreement that gave Indians in the province self-government.

After the end of World War II in 1945, the population of southern Ontario continued to grow. Thousands of Italian, Asian, Caribbean, and eastern European immigrants have settled in southern Ontario's large cities. Northern Ontario, which has grown more slowly, has attracted people from Italy, Finland, Ukraine, Poland, and Germany.

Northern Ontario is also home to many Native peoples. These Indians have long wanted a strong role in making decisions about their land and their resources. In 1991 a group of Indian leaders, along with Ontario's government, signed the Statement of Political Relationship. This agreement gave Indian nations in the province the right to govern themselves.

With more people than any other Canadian province, Ontario has a tough job trying to meet the needs of all of its different residents. But whether they live on a reserve, in a crowded city, or in a small mining or lumber town, Ontarians are proud to call this vast province home.

New guards slowly march in to replace the old ones during the traditional changing of the guard (above). *The ceremony is performed outside of Ontario's Parliament Buildings* (left) *each day during the summer.*

Canada's Industrial Heartland

Traveling north to south through Ontario, you can see the province's many industries. Tourism thrives in the north, where visitors come to hunt, fish, and explore the wilderness. Abundant forests, rich mines, and busy pulp and paper mills cover the land. To the south lie fertile farms and bustling cities, where people work in steel mills, car factories, and government offices.

Ontario's location in the heart of the nation helps the province's businesses do well. Companies in Ontario trade goods with the Prairie Provinces to the west and with the Atlantic Provinces to the east. Ontario's businesses send products through the Great Lakes to nations overseas. Directly across the Great Lakes lies a leading trade partner for Ontario and for all of Canada—the United States.

Ontario's natural resources include rich soil (facing page), ***vast forests*** (above), ***and a wealth of rivers*** (left). ***The rivers provide hydropower as well as trade routes for Ontario's goods.***

43

Construction is an important part of Ontario's service industry. Construction workers build homes, apartments, offices, and other buildings.

Many Ontarians play an important role in getting the province's goods to market. They have jobs in trade, which is part of the service industry. Workers in the service industry help out people and businesses. Some service workers, for example, sell mining products to foreign countries. Others load huge ships with Ontario's goods or guide freighters through locks along the Saint Lawrence Seaway.

The service industry provides jobs for about 76 percent of working Ontarians. These workers include bankers, teachers, doctors, lawyers, and government employees. Some people in the service industry help tourists by guiding tours or by greeting people at Ontario's provincial parks. Tourism earns a lot of money for Ontario.

While services make the most money for Ontario, a large portion of Ontario's earnings comes from manufacturing. About 19 percent of working Ontarians have jobs in factories or mills. In fact, Ontario is Canada's leader in manufacturing.

Many factories are located in an area called the Golden Horseshoe in southern Ontario. This industrial region curves around the western shore of Lake Ontario. Here workers assemble cars, trucks, buses, and airplanes. In nearby Ottawa, factory workers produce computers and computer parts.

Workers also turn raw materials such as fish, crops, minerals, and timber into finished products. Timber, for example, is sent to mills where it is ground into pulp for paper and newsprint or sawed into lumber. Meat, fruits, and vegetables are packaged in Ontario's many food-processing plants.

One of Ontario's leading industries is car manufacturing. The automobiles are sold all across Canada.

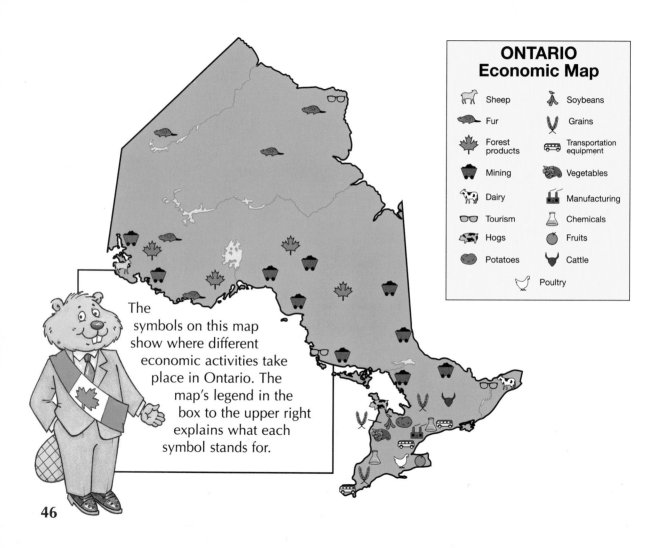

ONTARIO
Economic Map

Sheep

Soybeans

Fur

Grains

Forest products

Transportation equipment

Mining

Vegetables

Dairy

Manufacturing

Tourism

Chemicals

Hogs

Fruits

Potatoes

Cattle

Poultry

The symbols on this map show where different economic activities take place in Ontario. The map's legend in the box to the upper right explains what each symbol stands for.

In the fertile soil of southern Ontario, farmers grow vegetables, grains, and tobacco. Peach orchards, pumpkin patches, and grape vineyards dot the southern region. Corn, Ontario's main crop, feeds the province's cattle, hogs, and chickens. Altogether, farmers make up 4 percent of Ontario's workforce.

Nowadays Ontario's farms are larger, have more high-tech machinery, and produce more crops than ever before.

The farms in southern Ontario depend on the region's mild weather and rich soil. But factories and other businesses are also attracted to southern Ontario and compete for space with these farms. So farmers have to use their land efficiently to make farming worthwhile. To keep the soil healthy, farmers limit the use of fertilizers, which contain chemicals that can harm soil.

As Ontario's cities and suburbs spread across the south, they take over some of the province's farmland.

Officials work to make sure that loggers do not cut too many trees.

Ontarians also carefully manage their forests. The forests are harvested by the logging industry, which employs less than 1 percent of Ontario's workforce. Loggers cut down the province's fir, spruce, pine, cedar, and maple trees.

Logging companies must obey laws that protect the forests. The government places limits on the number of trees that logging businesses are allowed to take and requires that new seedlings be planted to replace cut trees. By following these laws, Ontarians make sure that enough timber is saved for wildlife habitat and for the logging industry.

Another industry that depends on a steady supply of natural resources is mining. Although mining provides jobs for less than 1 percent of working Ontarians, the mining industry makes a lot of money for Ontario. Workers in northern towns unearth nickel and copper, two of the province's major minerals. Gold, silver, and iron ore are mined, too. Southern Ontario's miners quarry salt and drill for oil.

Unlike trees, minerals cannot be replaced once they are removed from the earth. When mining companies use up a mineral supply, they try to find deposits in other areas of Ontario. Without new mines, the companies would go out of business.

To increase their earnings, Ontario's mining companies try to unearth minerals as efficiently as they can. Many firms use machines that dig at a steady rate, reducing the amount of energy and people needed for the job. But as high-tech machinery replaces people, some miners find themselves out of work.

Workers in this mine in northern Ontario (left) *dig for base metals such as nickel and copper. A gold miner* (above) *prepares an underground site for blasting.*

51

Working Underground

Eric is a nickel miner in the city of Sudbury, where Canada's largest nickel deposits are found. Each day, along with other miners, Eric rides an elevator called a cage deep below the ground. The miners wear rubber boots, safety glasses, and hard hats. Special lamps on the hats help brighten the darkness. Workers take breaks in underground lunchrooms that have hot plates and refrigerators.

On the job, Eric drives a scoop tram—a big truck with oversized tires and a large scoop in front. He thinks his job is a lot like driving above the ground, except that he does not have to worry about traffic or bad weather. Eric scoops up chunks of ore (a mix of minerals) that have been blasted loose from the earth. After driving the loaded tram through a tunnel, he dumps the ore into a crusher that breaks the material into small pieces.

The ore is hauled to the surface and sent to a mill to be ground into a very fine powder and cleaned with water and chemicals. The product then goes to a smelter, where heat from large furnaces removes other wastes. What comes out is pure nickel that can be used to produce items such as coins and jet engines.

The products from mining, logging, and farming are eventually sold to Canadians or to people in other countries. Because so many of the jobs in Ontario depend on these industries, Ontarians are concerned about preserving the province's natural resources. With proper management, natural resources will provide Ontario with jobs and money for years to come.

Ontario's natural resources are a source of scenic beauty as well as income.

Children wave flags bearing the nation's symbol—the maple leaf—to honor their Canadian heritage.

A Mix of Cultures

Ontario, the wealthiest and fastest-growing province in Canada, has a wide mix of people and cultures. Since the 1700s, immigrants have come to Ontario to start new lives. Some traveled to the far north and west to settle in the wilderness. But most people chose to live in the bustling towns and cities of southern Ontario.

Most of Ontario's 10 million people still live in the province's southern cities, which include Toronto, Ottawa, Windsor, and Hamilton. Northern Ontario, home to far fewer people, has some city dwellers, too. Cities in this region include Thunder Bay, Sudbury, and Sault Sainte Marie.

Boats line the shores of Lake Ontario's Toronto Island—a place where cars are not allowed.

55

Many inhabitants of northern Ontario live in towns that are scattered across the land. Most of these towns surround a mill or factory, where the majority of the residents work. Other northern residents live in small villages, where they make a living by fishing, raising mink on fur farms, or trapping fur-bearing animals. The most remote areas of the north can be reached only by taking a boat, train, or floatplane (a seaplane that lands on the water).

Whether they're from the north or the south, about one-fourth of Ontario's residents have British roots. Others also have European backgrounds, including French, German, and Italian.

A bagpiper wearing a traditional bearskin cap celebrates his Scottish heritage.

Many Ontarians live in the communities originally settled by their ancestors. Some Italians, for example, headed toward northwestern Ontario and to Toronto, where Italian communities still thrive. Large numbers of Ukrainians and Finns have settled in Thunder Bay and Sault Sainte Marie. Peoples of Portuguese and German ancestry make their homes around the Golden Horseshoe.

Large numbers of northern Ontarians live in the city of Thunder Bay, which is located on the western shore of Lake Superior.

French people from Québec settled around Sudbury, Timmins, and other northern towns. Many of these French-speaking settlers became miners or loggers and set up communities. Called Francophones, these residents speak mainly French but also know English. French schools, businesses, and churches are found in these areas.

Some Francophones feel that their heritage is ignored by English speakers who also live in these areas. Since the 1980s, large numbers of French speakers have left Ontario and moved to Québec, where French people are the majority and French is the main language. Even so, about 5 percent of Ontario's population is French.

Although many of Ontario's residents have European roots, other groups are getting larger. Since World War II, thousands of newcomers from other places have settled in Ontario's cities. Immigrants from the Caribbean, India, and eastern Asia live in Toronto and in other urban areas.

Among Ontario's newest immigrants are people from Asian nations.

A young dancer performs at a powwow.

About 126,000 Ontarians, or roughly 1 percent of the population, belong to Native nations. Half of these people live on the province's reserves. Many Cree and Ojibwa make their homes on reserves, fishing and trapping animals as their ancestors did. Logging, harvesting wild rice, and growing cranberries also bring earnings to Indian families. In recent years, many young adults have moved from the reserves to cities to find better-paying jobs.

Ontarians across the province celebrate their cultures. In northern Ontario, some Indians make traditional jewelry and crafts. Native peoples also hold powwows, where they perform the dances of their ancestors. Finnish dancers in the north perform folk dances. Ukrainian mandolin players strum songs from their homeland.

Southern Ontario's blend of cultures comes across in everyday life and in special events. In Toronto's ethnic neighborhoods, restaurants and markets have specialty foods from Asia and other regions of the world. Some restaurants feature tropical foods such as the plantain, a fruit that looks like a banana and is cooked before being eaten. Many street names appear in foreign languages, such as Italian or Chinese, as well as in English.

Yearly festivals celebrate various ethnic backgrounds with music, food, and dancing. In Toronto, Caribbean peoples host an event called Caribana, which attracts almost one million people each year. During Caribana, reggae music fills the air and dancers parade in colorful costumes.

Ottawa's annual Franco-Ontarian Festival highlights French culture with acrobats and crafts. Germans from Kitchener and Waterloo, twin cities in Ontario that share a German heritage, celebrate Oktoberfest. During this festival, German beer and polka bands are traditions. In Toronto's annual Metro International Caravan, booths all across the city showcase the art, crafts, and foods of many cultures.

Ontarians from all different backgrounds love sports. In winter, people go skiing or zoom along snowmobile trails. Nearly every town has a hockey team, and many young skaters dream of playing for the Toronto Maple Leafs. With the coming of spring, thousands of baseball fans cheer on the world champion Toronto Blue Jays. Summer is a favorite season for Ontario's canoeists and hikers.

Dressed in dazzling colors, a parader hopes to win a prize for best costume during the festival known as Caribana.

Ontarians also enjoy the arts. Toronto is home to the National Ballet of Canada. The city's many theaters feature plays, orchestras, choirs, or dance groups of all kinds. In the small southwestern town of Stratford, actors put on plays by William Shakespeare during the Stratford Festival. Residents of northern Ontario enjoy productions by the Sudbury Theatre Centre.

Ontario, with more cities and more people than any other province, continues to grow. The province's central location and thriving industries draw new residents each day. With its rugged wilderness, bustling cities, and ethnic mix, Ontario offers a little bit of everything.

Canoeing in Algonquin Park

Downtown Toronto

Baseball at the SkyDome

Cree Indian boys

Famous Ontarians

1 **Margaret Atwood** (born 1939), from Ottawa, is a novelist and poet. Atwood has received high praise for her poetry collection *The Circle Game* and for novels such as *The Handmaid's Tale*.

2 **Dan Aykroyd** (born 1952), a comedian and screenwriter from Ottawa, began his career in Toronto's Second City comedy troupe. Aykroyd gained fame on the TV show *Saturday Night Live* and later starred in many films, including *The Blues Brothers* and *Ghostbusters*.

3 **John Candy** (1950–1994) got his start in comedy with the Second City troupe in his hometown of Toronto. Candy later played comic parts in the TV programs *Second City TV* and *SCTV Network 90*. He is famous for roles in many movies, including *Uncle Buck* and *Cool Runnings*.

4 **Raffi Cavoukian** (born 1948) is originally from Egypt but grew up in Toronto. Known by his first name, Raffi is one of the most popular children's recording artists in Canada and the United States. His videos and his albums, such as *Singable Songs for the Very Young*, have won many awards.

5 **Wayne Gretzky** (born 1961), a world-famous hockey star from Brantford, Ontario, began skating for the Edmonton Oilers in his teens. This record-breaking player led his team to win the 1984 Stanley Cup and has received many awards, including the Hart Memorial Trophy and the Art Ross Trophy. In 1988 Gretzky joined the Los Angeles Kings.

7

■ **Josiah Henson** (1789–1883) was born a slave but escaped from the United States to what is now Dresden, Ontario, in 1830. There he founded a settlement for ex-slaves. Experts believe that the character of Uncle Tom in Harriet Beecher Stowe's famous novel *Uncle Tom's Cabin* was based on Henson's life.

7 **Adelaide Hoodless** (1857–1910) was born in Saint George, Canada West (now Ontario). After her baby son died from drinking impure milk, she supported a movement to teach women about motherhood and managing a home. Hoodless helped found Canadian organizations such as the National Council of Women and the national YWCA.

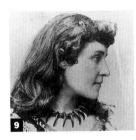

9

8 **Ferguson Jenkins** (born 1943), from Chatham, Ontario, has been called the best baseball player born in Canada. This former pitcher played for the Chicago Cubs and the Texas Rangers, among other teams. He was elected to the Canadian Baseball Hall of Fame in 1987.

9 **Pauline Johnson** (1862–1913), a poet from Ontario, was the daughter of a Six Nations chief and a British mother. Dressed as an Indian princess, Johnson read and performed her poems to audiences across Canada and overseas. Her works include *Canadian Born*.

8

10 **Karen Kain** (born 1951) is a ballerina originally from Hamilton, Ontario. She joined the National Ballet of Canada in 1969 and soon became the company's principal dancer. Kain has danced the leading role in many performances, including *Swan Lake, Giselle,* and *The Nutcracker.*

11 **Thomas Longboat** (1887–1949), an Indian from the Six Nations Reserve, was a celebrated long-distance runner. The record-breaking athlete won many Canadian races and took first place in the Boston Marathon of 1907.

10

11

12 **Sir John A. Macdonald** (1815–1891) was a lawyer in what is now Kingston, Ontario, before becoming the first prime minister of Canada in 1867. The leading spokesman for Confederation, Macdonald helped link the nation through the building of railroads and industries.

■ **William Lyon Mackenzie** (1795–1861), a Scottish newspaper editor in Upper Canada (now Ontario), became Toronto's first mayor in 1834. Opposed to British rule in Upper Canada, he led a failed rebellion against the government in 1837.

14 **Agnes Macphail** (1890–1954), a native of Proton Township, Ontario, was the first woman elected to Canada's House of Commons in 1921. She entered politics to support farmers' issues but quickly became interested in women's rights. In 1951 Macphail led Ontario's lawmakers to grant women equal pay in the workplace.

■ **Susanna Moodie** (1803–1885) moved with her husband from Britain to Ontario in 1832 to start a farm. After years of struggle, she wrote a book about the hardships of pioneer life called *Roughing It in the Bush*. Her follow-up to that classic story was titled *Life in the Clearings*.

■ **Farley Mowat** (born 1921) began writing at the age of six and has since penned many popular books, including *People of the Deer* and *Never Cry Wolf*. Mowat's works have been published in more than 40 countries. He was born in Belleville, Ontario.

17 **Robert Munsch** (born 1945), a resident of Guelph, Ontario, is an oral storyteller and a children's book writer. His picture books include *Love You Forever, The Paper Bag Princess,* and *Thomas' Snowsuit*.

18 **Christopher Plummer** (born 1929), an actor from Toronto, has starred in movies, TV shows, and Shakespearean plays. In 1973 he won a Tony Award for his performance in the musical *Cyrano*. Plummer is well known for his role as Captain von Trapp in the movie *The Sound of Music*.

19 **Keanu Reeves** (born 1965) grew up in Toronto. Most famous for his starring role as Ted in the movie *Bill and Ted's Excellent Adventure*, he has appeared in many other films, including *Parenthood* and *Speed*.

■ **Morley Safer** (born 1931), a longtime cohost on the news program *60 Minutes*, is from Toronto. Safer moved to the United States in 1964 to cover the Vietnam War and since then has received many awards for his work in broadcast journalism.

21 **Emily Stowe** (1831–1903), from Norwich in Upper Canada (now Ontario), wanted to be a doctor. But in her day, no colleges in Canada enrolled women. After receiving a degree from the New York Medical College for Women, she returned to Canada to practice medicine and to fight for women's rights.

22 **Michelle Wright** (born 1961) is a well-known country music star from Chatham, Ontario. In 1990 she won the Canadian Country Music Association award for best female singer and has received many other honors. One of her biggest hit songs is "Take It Like a Man."

23 **Neil Young** (born 1945), a guitarist and singer, recorded with groups such as Buffalo Springfield and Crosby, Stills, Nash, and Young. Young has made many successful solo albums, including *After the Gold Rush* and *Harvest Moon*. He was born in Toronto.

Fast Facts

Provincial Symbols

Motto: *Ut Incepit Fidelis sic Permanet* (Loyal it began, loyal it remains)
Flower: white trillium
Tree: eastern white pine
Bird: common loon
Gem: amethyst
Tartan: the colors are from Ontario's coat of arms—yellow for the maple leaves, red for the Cross of Saint George, black for the bear, and brown for the moose and deer.

Provincial Highlights

Landmarks: Old Fort William in Thunder Bay, National Gallery of Canada in Ottawa, Algonquin Park in southern Ontario, Ontario Place in Toronto, Canada's Wonderland in Maple, Joseph Brant Museum in Burlington, Polar Bear Express in Cochrane

Annual events: Spring Festival in Guelph (May), International Children's Festival in London (June), Fun in the Sun Festival in Fort Frances (June), Canadian National Exhibition in Toronto (Aug.–Sept.), Niagara Grape & Wine Festival in Saint Catharines (Sept.), Winter Festival of Lights in Niagara Falls (Nov.–Jan.)

Professional sports teams: Toronto Blue Jays (baseball); Toronto Maple Leafs (hockey); Hamilton Tiger-Cats, Ottawa Rough Riders, Toronto Argonauts (football); Toronto Raptors (basketball)

Population

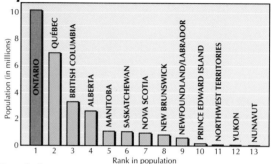

Population*: 10,085,000
Rank in population, nationwide: 1st
Population distribution: 82 percent urban; 18 percent rural
Population density: 28.5 people per sq mi (11 per sq km)
Capital: Toronto (3,893,000—metro area)
Major cities (and populations*): Hamilton (318,499), Ottawa (313,987), London (310,000), Windsor (192,822), Kitchener (170,638), Thunder Bay (113,946), Sudbury (92,884)
Major ethnic groups*: Multiple backgrounds, 56 percent; British, 25 percent; French, 5 percent; Italian, 5 percent; German, 3 percent; Dutch and Polish, 2 percent each; Ukrainian, 1 percent; North American Indian, Métis, Inuit, 1 percent total

*1991 census

68

Endangered Species

Mammals: eastern cougar
Birds: anatum peregrine falcon, piping plover, logger-head shrike, Henslow's sparrow, Kirtland's warbler
Amphibians: Blanchard's cricket frog
Reptiles: blue racer snake, Lake Erie water snake
Fish: aurora trout
Plants: eastern prickly pear cactus, Skinner's agalinis, slender bush clover, white prairie gentian, small white lady's slipper, pink milkwort, hoary mountain-mint, heart-leaved plantain, wood poppy

Geographic Highlights

Area (land/water): 412,579 sq mi (1,068,580 sq km)
Rank in area, nationwide: 4th
Highest point: Ishpatina Ridge (2,274 ft/693 m)
Major lakes: Superior, Huron, Erie, Ontario, Nipigon, Lake of the Woods, Seul, Abitibi, Nipissing

Economy
Percentage of Workers Per Job Sector:

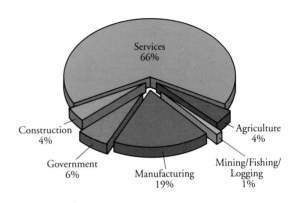

Services 66%
Construction 4%
Government 6%
Manufacturing 19%
Mining/Fishing/Logging 1%
Agriculture 4%

Natural resources: water, forests, fertile soil, nickel, uranium, copper, gold, silver, zinc, iron ore, oil, natural gas, salt
Agricultural products: corn, wheat, barley, soybeans, hogs, beef and dairy cattle, eggs, poultry, fruits and vegetables
Manufactured goods: automobiles, aircraft, railcars, computers, paper, steel

Energy

Electric power: nuclear power (50 percent), hydroelectric (25 percent), fuel-burning (25 percent)

69

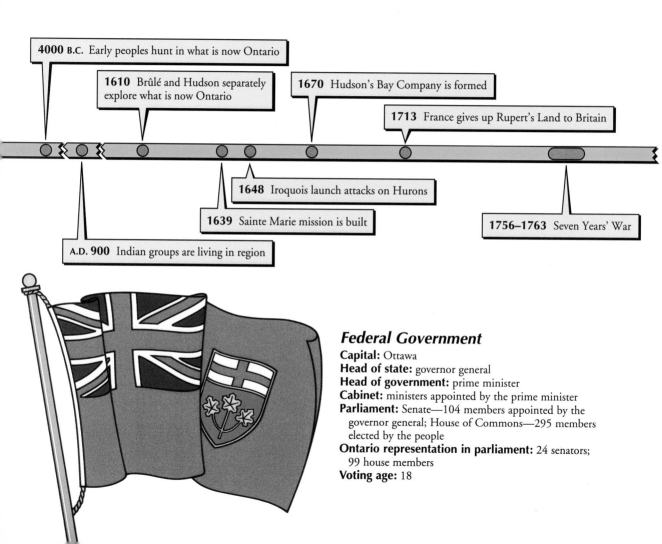

4000 B.C. Early peoples hunt in what is now Ontario

1610 Brûlé and Hudson separately explore what is now Ontario

1670 Hudson's Bay Company is formed

1713 France gives up Rupert's Land to Britain

1648 Iroquois launch attacks on Hurons

1639 Sainte Marie mission is built

1756–1763 Seven Years' War

A.D. 900 Indian groups are living in region

Federal Government

Capital: Ottawa
Head of state: governor general
Head of government: prime minister
Cabinet: ministers appointed by the prime minister
Parliament: Senate—104 members appointed by the governor general; House of Commons—295 members elected by the people
Ontario representation in parliament: 24 senators; 99 house members
Voting age: 18

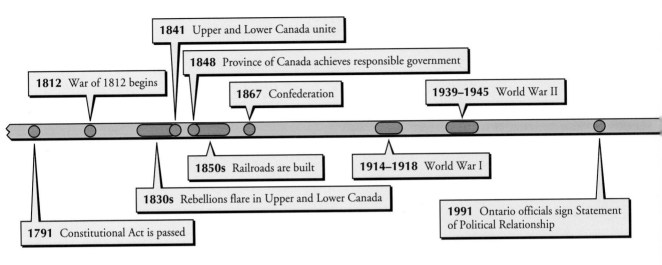

1841 Upper and Lower Canada unite

1848 Province of Canada achieves responsible government

1812 War of 1812 begins

1867 Confederation

1939–1945 World War II

1850s Railroads are built

1914–1918 World War I

1830s Rebellions flare in Upper and Lower Canada

1991 Ontario officials sign Statement of Political Relationship

1791 Constitutional Act is passed

Provincial Government

Capital: Toronto
Head of state: lieutenant governor
Head of government: premier
Cabinet: ministers appointed by the premier
Legislative Assembly: 130 members elected to terms that can last up to five years
Voting age: 18
Major political parties: Progressive Conservative, Liberal, New Democratic

Government Services

To help pay the people who work for Ontario's government, Ontarians pay taxes on money they earn and on many of the items they buy. The services run by the provincial government assure Ontarians of a high quality of life. The government pays for medical care, for education, for road building and repairs, and for other facilities such as libraries and parks. In addition, the government has funds to help people who are disabled, elderly, or poor.

71

Glossary

colony   A territory ruled by a country some distance away.

Confederation   The union of four British colonies under the British North America Act in 1867. Confederation formed the Dominion of Canada and set up two levels of government—national and provincial. Other provinces later joined the original four.

glacier   A large body of ice and snow that moves slowly over land.

Great Lakes   A chain of five lakes bordering Canada and the United States. They are Lakes Superior, Michigan, Huron, Erie, and Ontario.

hydropower   The electricity produced by using the force of flowing water. Also called hydroelectric power.

immigrant   A person who moves into a foreign country and settles there.

lock   An enclosed, water-filled chamber in a canal or river used to raise or lower the water level so boats can travel beyond a waterfall. Boats can enter the lock through gates at either end.

Loyalist   A person who supports the government during a revolt.

missionary   A person sent out by a religious group to spread its beliefs.

muskeg   A mossy bog often found in northern Canada that contains thick layers of decayed vegetable matter.

permafrost   Ground that remains frozen for two or more years.

reserve Public land set aside by the government to be used by Native peoples.

responsible government A form of government that made the governor responsible (answerable) to an assembly elected by the people.

treaty An agreement between two or more groups, usually having to do with peace or trade.

Pronunciation Guide

Algonquian (al-GAHN-kwee-uhn)

Brûlé, Étienne (broo-LAY, ay-TYEHN)

Champlain, Samuel de
(shaw^n-PLA^n, sah-myoo-EHL duh)

des Groseilliers, Médard Chouart
(day groh-zeh-YAY, may-DAHR shoo-WAHR)

Iroquoian (IHR-uh-kwoy-uhn)

Manitoulin (man-uh-TOO-luhn)

Ottawa (AHT-uh-wuh)

Peterborough (PEET-uh-buhr-uh)

Radisson, Pierre-Esprit
(rah-dee-SOH^n, pee-EHR ehs-PREE)

Sault Sainte Marie
(SOO SAYNT muh-REE)

Toronto (tuh-RAHNT-oh)

Index ▬▬▬

About the Author

Originally from London, England, Michael Barnes has lived in northeastern Ontario since 1956. He began writing during his 34-year career as an elementary schoolteacher and principal. Now a full-time author, Barnes has written more than 30 books, mostly about northern Ontario and about police work. He also presents readings and workshops for arts councils and broadcasts regularly for the CBC Radio-Northern network.

Acknowledgments

Laura Westlund, pp. 1, 3, 24 (right), 31, 52, 68–71; Jim West/Impact Visuals, pp. 2, 55, 62, 73; CN Tower, p. 6; Terry Boles, 7, 10, 46, 69; Peterborough & Kawarthas Tourism & Convention Bureau, p. 7; Diane Cooper, pp. 8, 41 (inset); Mapping Specialists Ltd., pp. 10–11, 46; © Piotrek B. Gorski, pp. 12, 44, 63 (top right); ON Ministry of Natural Resources, p. 13; David Dvorak, Jr., p. 14; Industry, Science, and Technology Canada, pp. 15, 45, 48 (right), 54, 56, 57, 59, 61; St. Lawrence Seaway Authority, pp. 16, 43 (left); © James P. Rowan, p. 17, 20; Winston Fraser, p. 18; Rob & Melissa Simpson, p. 19; Nat'l Archives of Canada, pp. 20 (inset/C38943), 22 (C45487), 29 (C70260), 30 (C3904), 32 (PA11566), 35 (C4806), 36–37 (C14114), 38 (left/C38828), 65 (top left/PA128887); Frederick S. Challener, *Étienne Brûlé at the Mouth of the Humber, 1615,* Gov't of ON Art Coll./Tom Moore Photography, Toronto, p. 23; Lib. of Congress, p. 24 (left); Bettmann Archive, p. 25; Hudson's Bay Co. Archives, Provincial Archives of MB, pp. 27, 33; Metropolitan Toronto Ref. Lib., p. 28; Nat'l Gallery of Canada, p. 34; Archives of ON, pp. 37 (bottom/6920–S12663), 65 (middle left/5898), 66 (top left/S271–1582, top right/A02027), 67 (middle left/S17839–2802); City of Toronto Archives, p. 38 (right/RG8–32–48); Thunder Bay Historical Museum Society, p. 39 (994,124.41); ON Native Affairs, p. 40; Jerry Hennen, p. 41 (left); ON Ministry of Agriculture, Food & Rural Affairs, p. 42; © John D. Stradiotto, pp. 43 (right), 47; © Bert Schmid, p. 48 (left); © Queen's Printer for ON, 1994, reproduced with permission, pp. 49, 51 (inset), 74; Falconbridge Ltd., pp. 50–51, 52; Jon Nelson, p. 53; Ottawa Tourism and Convention Authority, p. 58; Toronto Blue Jays, p. 63 (left); Lucille Sukalo, p. 63 (bottom right); Hollywood Book & Poster, pp. 64 (top left, middle right), 67 (top left, top right); Laurence Acland, p. 64 (top right); Colin Goldie/GM Studios, Vancouver, p. 64 (middle left); Los Angeles Kings, p. 64 (bottom); Nat'l Baseball Lib., Cooperstown, N.Y., p. 65 (middle right); Nat'l Ballet of Canada, p. 65 (bottom left); Boston Public Lib., Print Dept., p. 65 (bottom right); Annick Press, p. 66 (bottom left); Mike Hashimoto, p. 67 (bottom left); Savannah Music, Inc., p. 67 (bottom right).